Algy's Amazing Adventures

IN

SPACE

Look out for

Algy's Amazing Adventures

IN

Kaye Umansky

Illustrated by
Richard Watson

Orion
Children's Books

First published in Great Britain in 2014
by Orion Children's Books
a division of the Orion Publishing Group Ltd
Orion House
5 Upper St Martin's Lane
London WC2H 9EA
An Hachette UK company

1 3 5 7 9 10 8 6 4 2

Text © Kaye Umansky 2014
Illustrations © Richard Watson 2014

The right of Kaye Umansky and Richard Watson to be identified
as author and illustrator of this work has been asserted.

All rights reserved. No part of this publication may
be reproduced, stored in a retrieval system, or transmitted,
in any form or by any means, electronic, mechanical,
photocopying, recording, or otherwise, without the prior
permission of Orion Children's Books.

The Orion Publishing Group's policy is to use papers that
are natural, renewable and recyclable products and made
from wood grown in sustainable forests. The logging and
manufacturing processes are expected to conform to the
environmental regulations of the country of origin.

A catalogue record for this book is available
from the British Library.

ISBN 978 1 4440 0690 2

Printed and bound in China

www.orionbooks.co.uk

For Ivy Rose

Contents

Chapter One

This is Algy. Most of the time, he lives a normal life, in a normal house with a normal garden.

But at the bottom of Algy's garden is a shed. In that shed is a loose plank. And behind that plank is . . .

Another world!

This is Cherry from next door.
She always comes along when
Algy has adventures.

This is Brad, Cherry's little brother. He thinks adventures are fun!

Algy was in a bad mood. He wanted to meet Cherry for an adventure, but his mum was making him tidy his room.

"It's a mess," she said.

"I can't help it," said Algy. "I need more space. I hate tidying. It's boring."

"Tough," said his mum.

Algy waited until his mum
had disappeared into her
bedroom, then crept downstairs
and out into the garden.

Cherry and Brad were waiting in the shed.

"Let's see what's behind the plank," said Cherry.

With a little thrill of
excitement Algy gave the plank a
push. And through the gap they
saw . . .

"Oh wow!" gasped Algy.

Chapter Two

Algy was looking at a very strange world indeed.

He had a book called *The Universe*. In it there were lots of pictures of the surface of the moon and Mars.

Were they in space? On another planet? Cool! Algy had always wanted to be an astronaut.

"Creepy," said Cherry. "You go first, Algy."

The first thing Algy noticed when he squeezed through the gap was that his body felt lighter. He gave a little jump – and rose into the air.

But he didn't thump back
down. He floated gently, like a
feather. He had seen pictures of
astronauts doing this. It was all to
do with something called gravity.

"Look!" shouted Algy. "Come on, have a go!"

Cherry and Brad followed him. They jumped high into the air too.

"I'm flying!" shouted Cherry.

"Funny!" yelled Brad.

Algy was having so much fun that at first he didn't notice the small dust cloud coming towards them.

"Yap-yap-yap! Yap-yap-yap!" it went.

The dust cloud screeched to a halt at Algy's feet. There, staring up at him, panting loudly, was a dog.

Well, it *looked* like a dog. It had legs and ears and a tail. But it seemed to be made entirely of shiny silver metal.

"Yap!" barked the dog. "Yap!"

Algy didn't like strange dogs.
This one was the strangest he'd
ever met.

"Don't touch it!" he said
to Cherry. "Back away slowly.
Towards the shed."

But Brad had other ideas.

"Tin doggy," said Brad.
"Tinny." He reached forward and
patted the dog's head. A long,
silver tongue popped out and
licked him on the nose.

"Ah, look at that," said
Cherry. "It's cute."

She reached forward too – but
then the dog opened its jaws and
grabbed her jumper.

"Hey!" said Cherry.

The dog let go, then it turned and ran a short way. It stopped, looked back at Algy, and whined. It ran on a few more paces – then stopped again.

"I think it wants us to go with it," said Algy.

"Yap!" barked Tinny. "Yap!"

There are two things we can do, thought Algy. We can go back to the shed, or we can follow. What would an astronaut do?

"Right," said Algy. "Let's go."

Chapter Three

Tinny didn't bounce like they
did. It raced along the ground,
kicking up dust with its paws.

Algy, Cherry and Brad
bounced behind it, trying to
avoid the odd, round holes in the
dusty ground.

"Don't land in the holes,
Brad," shouted Cherry.

There was a big one just in front, so Algy made an extra high jump. He looked up, and beyond the rocks he caught a glimpse of a huge, glass dome.

Whatever could that be?

As they got closer to the rocks, Algy saw something else. There was a strange-looking vehicle parked at the edge of a deep, steep-sided hole.

Tinny raced to the edge of the
hole. It held up a paw and gave a
little whimper.

Lying flat out at the bottom of
the hole was . . .

"A robot!" gasped Algy.

Just like Tinny, the robot was made of metal. It had jointed arms and legs and a square head with circles for eyes and a slit for a mouth.

It wasn't moving.

"Say something," whispered Cherry. "Go on."

"Hey!" called Algy. "Are you all right?"

There was a pause. Then the robot spoke. Its voice sounded very weak, and Algy could only just hear what it was saying.

"Rope . . . in buggy . . . hurry . . ."

There was no time to lose. Algy needed to think quickly, like an astronaut.

"You look for the rope, Cherry," said Algy. "I'll go down and see what I can do."

Algy stepped into the hole and floated to the bottom. He didn't think it was dangerous, but you never could tell.

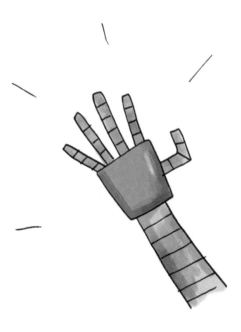

Chapter Four

Algy crouched by the robot.

"Hello," he said. "What's wrong?"

"Flat . . . batteries," said the robot. "Need charge . . . too heavy."

Oh no, thought Algy. The robot must be too heavy to bounce like we can.

Cherry appeared at the top of the hole with a length of rope.

"Here!" she shouted. "Catch!"

Algy took the rope and made a loop. He slipped it over the robot's head, down over its shoulders, and then pulled it tight under the armpits.

"Right," said Algy. "Hold on. We'll have you out in no time."

He sprang up and floated out of the hole.

"Time to pull, everyone," he said.

They all took their places at the rope. Even Tinny.

"On the count of three," said Algy. "One, two, three – pull!"

The robot was heavier than Algy expected. He could hear it bumping and scraping against the side of the hole until, finally, its metal head appeared.

Algy and Cherry ran to help the robot to its feet.

"Buggy," gasped the robot. "Charger . . ."

They helped the robot to the buggy. It reached in, pulled out a long cord, then plugged the end into a socket in its belt.

The robot gave a jerk. Slowly, it straightened. It moved its head from side to side. It raised and lowered its arms. It flexed its knees. Then it gave a nod.

"Fully charged and ready for work," said the robot. Its voice sounded much stronger now. "Thank you, sir, and goodbye," it said. Then it opened the buggy door and Tinny jumped in.

"Wait!" said Algy.

"Yes, sir?" said the robot.

"What – I mean – *who* are you?" said Algy.

"I am GUS. Garden Utility Servo."

"My dog is FRISC. Faithful Robotic Intelligent Servo Companion."

"We called him Tinny," said Cherry. "But FRISC is lovely too."

"How did you fall down the hole?" asked Algy.

"I was walking FRISC and the ground gave way. I used up my batteries trying to climb out. I must go to work now, sir. The plants need water," said GUS.

"Plants?" said Algy. "What plants?"

"Under the dome," said GUS, pointing to the glass roof in the distance. "If you wish, I will show you."

"Yes, please," Algy said.

They all piled in the buggy.
GUS pulled a lever, and –
vroooom! They were off!

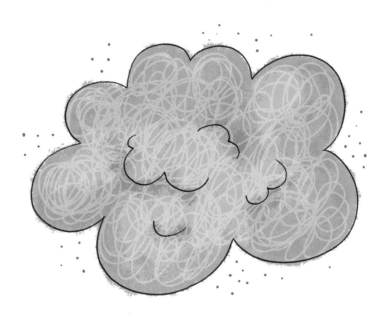

Chapter Five

Algy had never ridden so fast in his life. The buggy hardly seemed to touch the ground.

"Wheeeee!" screamed Brad.

"Yap! Yap!" barked FRISC.

The glass dome loomed before them, huge and gleaming in the strange red light.

The buggy pulled up outside and came to a halt.

"Follow me," said GUS.

He walked up to the dome and pointed a metal finger. A large glass panel moved smoothly to one side.

Algy's jaw dropped. He had
seen some odd looking plants,
but none like these.

"Funny twees," said Brad. His eyes were wide.

"What are they for, GUS?" asked Algy.

"Food," said GUS. "My masters eat the pods."

"What do they taste like?" asked Cherry.

"I do not know. Utility Servos do not eat," said GUS.

"Where are your masters now?" asked Algy.

GUS pointed to the black sky. "Away. Back soon," he said.

How soon is soon? wondered
Algy. Next week? Tomorrow?
Today?

"What are they like?" he asked.
"Are they like . . . us?"

"More legs," said GUS.
"Sharper teeth. Greener. Long tails."

Sharp teeth?

Green?

Tails?

Algy and Cherry looked at each other. Cherry took Brad's hand.

"I think we should go home now," she said.

"Yes," said Algy. "I think we should."

Chapter Six

That night, Algy lay in bed
thinking about the adventure.

GUS had given them a lift
back to the shed in his buggy.

As they'd zoomed along, he had pointed to a star shooting across the sky and said, "My masters are coming home!"

Sharp teeth. More legs. Green. Algy was very glad to see the shed.

Everyone was sad to say goodbye. GUS asked if they were sure they wouldn't stay and meet his masters.

All three of them said, "No, thank you."

It had been a wonderful adventure – but Algy had had enough space for one day. He was glad to be back in his tiny bedroom. It felt cosy and safe.

Algy thought about GUS, working in that big glass dome. Growing food for aliens. Food that he didn't even eat. How boring that must be. It was a good thing he had FRISC for company.

Tomorrow, thought Algy, I'll tidy my room without moaning.

What are you going to read next?

Have more adventures with Horrid Henry,

and travel the world with

Miranda the Explorer.

Play clever tricks with Twit,

spend Mondays at Monster School,

and even brave The Dragon's Dentist . . .

Learn how love is just like a Woolly Hat,

dance under The Little Nut Tree,

take home Monstar, the best pet ever,

and have an extra-special Mr Monkey birthday party!

Enjoy all the Early Readers.

the orion star

★ ★ ★

CALLING ALL GROWN-UPS!
Sign up for the orion star newsletter to
hear about your favourite authors and exclusive
competitions, plus details of how children
can join our 'Story Stars' review panel.

Sign up at:

www.orionbooks.co.uk/orionstar

Follow us 🐦 @the_orionstar
Find us 📘 facebook.com/TheOrionStar